KT-132-134

To Aleka, with love

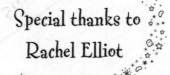

Special thanks to
Rachel Elliot

ORCHARD BOOKS

First published in Great Britain in 2017 by The Watts Publishing Group

1 3 5 7 9 10 8 6 4 2

© 2017 Rainbow Magic Limited.
© 2017 HIT Entertainment Limited.
Illustrations © Orchard Books 2017

HiT entertainment

A CIP catalogue record for this book is available from the British Library.

ISBN 978 1 40834 721 8

Printed and bound in Great Britain by CPI Group (UK) Ltd, Croydon, CR0 4YY

MIX
Paper from
responsible sources
FSC
www.fsc.org
FSC® C104740

The paper and board used in this book are made from wood from responsible sources

Orchard Books
An imprint of Hachette Children's Group
Part of The Watts Publishing Group Limited
Carmelite House, 50 Victoria Embankment, London EC4Y 0DZ

An Hachette UK Company
www.hachette.co.uk
www.hachettechildrens.co.uk

# Monica
# the Marshmallow
# Fairy

Join the **Rainbow Magic Reading Challenge**!

Read the story and collect your fairy points to climb the
Reading Rainbow at the back of the book.

This book is worth 5 points.

# Monica
# the Marshmallow
# Fairy

by Daisy Meadows

ORCHARD

www.rainbowmagic.co.uk

Jack Frost's
Ice Castle

Animal Shelter

Village
Hall

CHILDREN'S HOSPITAL

Children's
Hospital

# Jack Frost's Spell

Give me candy! Give me sweets!
Give me sticky, fizzy treats!
Lollipops and fudge so yummy -
Bring them here to fill my tummy.

Monica, I'll steal from you.
Gabby, Lisa, Shelley too.
I will build a sweetie shop,
So I can eat until I pop!

# Contents

# A Magical Invitation

"Welcome back to Wetherbury!" said Kirsty Tate.

Her best friend Rachel Walker placed a raspberry-coloured suitcase on Kirsty's bed.

"I'm so happy to be here with you for the week," she said. "I'll just unpack my things and then we can go and play."

As she reached out to open the suitcase, Mrs Tate came in holding the phone.

"It's your Aunt Harri," she told Kirsty.

Kirsty took the phone and Mrs Tate left the room. As Kirsty chatted to her aunt, a huge smile lit up her face, and Rachel hopped from foot to foot, longing to know what was being said. Aunt Harri worked at the Candy Land sweet factory outside the village, and Kirsty and Rachel thought that she might just have the best job in the world.

Kirsty hung up the phone and clapped her hands together.

"Rachel, Aunt Harri's going to be here any minute," she said, brimming with excitement. "She's going to pick us up in the Candy Land van for a special trip."

Rachel squealed, and the girls linked

hands and spun around
in delight.

"Do you think
she's going to take
us to the Candy
Land factory?"
Kirsty said.

"If she does, I
wonder if we'll see
the Sweet Fairies again,"
said Rachel.

She and Kirsty shared a happy smile.
The last time they had seen Aunt Harri,
they had been caught up in a magical
adventure with their fairy friends.
Because they had promised always
to keep the secrets of Fairyland, they
couldn't tell anyone else about their
adventures. It was always wonderful to

be able to talk about magic together.

Just then, Rachel's raspberry-coloured suitcase started to glow. The clasps rattled, and then the suitcase burst open and a tiny fairy fluttered out.

She was wearing a buttoned denim skirt, a fluffy jumper and pink sandals, and her shiny brown hair swished around her face.

"Hello, Rachel and Kirsty," she said. "I'm Monica the Marshmallow Fairy."

"It's amazing to meet you," said Kirsty.

"Welcome to Wetherbury ... but what are you doing here?"

"I'm one of the Candy Land Fairies," said Monica, perching on the open lid of the suitcase. "I'm here to take you to the Sweet Factory in Fairyland. The Candy Land Fairies are hoping to speak to you – will you come?"

The girls exchanged a look of sheer delight. They had been to the Sweet Factory before, and they knew that it was a magical place full of sweet fairy treats.

"Of course," they said together.

"We always love visiting Fairyland," Kirsty went on. "And luckily, time always stops in the human world while we're there, so we'll be back before Aunt Harri arrives to collect us."

"Great! I need you to sit on your bed, please," said Monica, smiling.

Kirsty and Rachel sat down beside the suitcase, and Monica raised her wand. A flurry of tiny pink marshmallows danced around the girls, and they saw fairy dust sparkling as they shrank to fairy size. Their wings unfurled and Monica fluttered down to join them.

"Hold hands, girls," she said. "Let's go to Fairyland."

There was a sudden, sweet smell in the air, and the tiny marshmallows danced faster and faster, lifting them into the air. Then Kirsty's bedroom disappeared and the swirl of marshmallows slowed down. As the last marshmallows disappeared, they saw that they were standing in the Fairyland Sweet Factory – an orchard of scrumptious-looking trees.

"Oh, I love it here," said Rachel, clapping her hands together. "I wish our garden had sweets growing on trees."

"Especially when there are always new sweets to enjoy," said another voice.

Three other fairies were standing in a clearing. When they saw Rachel and Kirsty, they smiled and fluttered their pastel-coloured wings.

"These are the other Candy Land Fairies," said Monica. "Gabby the Bubble Gum Fairy, Lisa the Jelly Bean Fairy and Shelley the Sherbet Fairy."

"What is your job?" asked Rachel.

Monica held out a sparkly pink marshmallow.

"Each of us has a magical sweet," said Monica. "We use them to make sure that all the candy in Fairyland and the human world is sweet and delicious."

The other fairies held out their hands too. Lisa had a glittering jelly bean. Gabby was holding a shiny strip of bubble gum and Shelley had a tube of sparkling sherbet.

"What a wonderful job," said Rachel, gazing around at the brightly coloured trees and smiling. "I think this might be

my favourite place in Fairyland."

"Of course, you already know about the Sweet Factory orchard," said Shelley. "You know many of our friends."

She waved at a group of fairies who were working at the far end of the orchard.

"It's the Sweet Fairies with Honey the Sweet Fairy and Lizzie the Sweet Treats Fairy," said Kirsty, also waving. "Oh, Monica, thank you so much for bringing us here again."

# Thieves in the Orchard

The beautiful Sweet Factory trees were
chock-full of humbugs, sherbet lemons,
chocolate mints, strawberry creams,
orange fondants and fudge squares, ready
to be picked. Monica fluttered over to a
marshmallow tree and plucked a bunch
of multi-coloured marshmallows for
Rachel and Kirsty to try.

"It's like eating little puffs of cloud," said Rachel. "They're so incredibly sweet and fluffy."

"The sweets are just reaching their best," said Monica. "They'll be ready to harvest in a few days. After the Candy Harvest, we'll have our traditional Harvest Feast – and that's why we asked you to come here today."

"We'd all like to invite you to attend the Harvest Feast," said Lisa. "Will you come with us?"

"We'd love to," said Kirsty, exchanging an excited grin with Rachel. "It sounds totally amazing."

But then they heard something that wiped their smiles away. A horrible

cackle echoed around
the orchard and Rachel
clutched Kirsty's hand
in alarm.

"That sounded like
Jack Frost!" she said.

Next moment, the
Ice Lord and his
goblins popped out
from behind the
trees around them.
They started shaking
the trees, and sweets
began to rain down
around them.

"No, stop!" cried
Gabby.

She darted forward, but
the goblins started pelting her

with sweets, squawking with laughter when she flew back to the others again.

"Stop throwing those sweeties!" Jack Frost bellowed at the goblins. "They're mine now – all mine!"

"They're not yours," Monica said bravely. "These sweets are meant to be shared by everyone who loves them."

"Fiddlesticks!" Jack Frost retorted. "No one loves sweeties more than I do. And no one except me is going to get any. I'm opening my own sweet shop at the Ice Castle, and only one customer will be allowed. ME!"

Without warning, the goblins charged towards the Candy Land Fairies and the fairies stumbled backwards. In their shock, they let go of their magical sweets. The goblins caught them and ran back to Jack Frost.

"Honey, Lizzie, help!" called Kirsty. "Sweet Fairies, help!"

The other fairies zoomed towards them from the other end of the orchard.

"You won't catch us!" the goblins squawked nastily.

Jack Frost waved his wand and there

was a flash of blue lightning and a clap
of thunder. Rachel kept her eyes fixed
on the Ice Lord and saw him shout
something, but the noise of the thunder
drowned out his voice. Then he and the
goblins vanished. Rachel and Kirsty
gazed around at the half-empty trees as
the other fairies reached them.

"They've caused so much damage," said
Honey with a groan. "Why does Jack
Frost do such horrible things?"

"He hasn't just damaged the trees,"
said Monica, fluttering over to stand
between Rachel and Kirsty. "He's taken
our magical sweets."

Honey, Lizzie and the Sweet Fairies
gasped in shock.

"Without them, all sweets everywhere
will taste horrible," said Lizzie. "Jack Frost

24

must be stopped."

"What are we going to do?" whispered Monica, with tears in her eyes.

"I've got an idea," said Rachel. "I saw Jack Frost shout something to the goblins just before he left. I couldn't hear him because of the thunder, but I was trying to read his lips. I'm sure he said

something about the human world. I
think he was telling his goblins to go
and hide there."

"It's a wonderful clue," asked Monica,
clasping her hands together. "Rachel
and Kirsty, if I come back to your world
with you, will you help me to look for
the goblins?"

The girls agreed at once, and Monica
turned to the other fairies.

"As soon as I have news, I will come
back," she said. "Now that I have Rachel
and Kirsty helping me, I'm sure that we
can stop Jack Frost's plans."

She lifted her wand and then swished
it through the air. Instantly, the girls
were human again and standing in
Kirsty's bedroom.

"Where shall we start looking?" asked

Monica, looking around.

Before the girls could reply, they heard
the sound of an engine outside the house.
Kirsty dashed to the window.

"It's Aunt Harri," she said. "Monica, my
aunt is taking us out for a surprise. Will
you come with us? We can keep our eyes
peeled for goblins as we go. She works
in a sweet factory — she might even be

taking us there."

"It sounds like a great way to start our search," said Monica.

She dived into Kirsty's pocket to hide and the girls hurried downstairs to greet Aunt Harri.

# Summer Snow

Kirsty threw open the front door and smiled when she saw her fair-haired young aunt.

"Hello, girls!" said Aunt Harri, giving them both a big hug. "I'm thrilled that you can join me for this very special trip. Hurry and get your shoes on – we have a short drive ahead of us."

"Where are we going?" asked Rachel, already filled with excitement.

Aunt Harri's blue eyes shone.

"Candy Land is rewarding village children with parcels of sweets for doing good deeds," she said. "The children have been nominated by their families and friends, who think that they deserve a special treat. We've called it Candy Land's Helping Hands, and I thought that you would like to come with me to surprise the first winner."

"That's a brilliant idea," said Kirsty. "I can't wait to see the first winner's face. Who is it?"

"It's a boy called Ori," said Aunt Harri. "He helps at the Treehouse Club, which runs camping trips and woodland activities for younger children."

"I know Ori from school," said Kirsty. "He's a nice boy."

"He's at the Treehouse Club today, getting ready for a camp-out this evening," said Aunt Harri as the girls called goodbye to Mrs Tate and left the house. "The plan is to surprise him around the campfire with a big bag of marshmallows. They're his favourites."

As the girls followed Aunt Harri out to the van, they exchanged an anxious glance with each other. Now that

Monica's magical marshmallow had been stolen, would all marshmallows everywhere taste horrible?

The girls climbed into the back of the van and saw a bulging Candy Land carrier bag on the seat. It had pink and white stripes, and *Candy Lane's Helping Hand* was written across the side in sparkly silver glitter. As Aunt Harri drove off, Kirsty leaned over and peeked inside.

"Oh no," she whispered.

Rachel peered into the bag and groaned. It should have been full of colourful

marshmallows, but they had all melted
into a big, gloopy mess.

"Ori won't enjoy those at all," she said.
"We have to find the goblins and get
Monica's marshmallow back before he
opens the magical bag."

Aunt Harri drove out of the village
and through twisty lanes until they came
to a wooded area. She parked the van
and the girls jumped out, leaving the bag
of marshmallows in the van. A young
man and woman strode towards them
out of the woods.

"Hi, Harri," said the woman. "Who do
we have here?"

"I'd like you to meet my niece Kirsty
and her best friend Rachel," said Aunt
Harri. "Girls, Carlotta and Calvin are
the leaders of the Treehouse Club. They're

also old friends of mine from school."

"Not *that* old," said Calvin with a grin.

The three adults laughed and started to talk about their school days. Rachel and Kirsty hovered in the background, not quite sure what to do. Carlotta noticed them and smiled.

"I'm sure you two don't want to listen to us giggling about what we did when we were your age," she said in a kind voice. "Why don't you go and look for Ori? Go along that path and it will take you straight to the treehouse. You'll find him and the others there."

She turned back to Calvin and Aunt Harri, and the girls set off along the wooded path that she had pointed out. The girls hurried along, enjoying the sound of the bracken cracking under their feet. Birds called to each other, and the scent of pine trees filled the air. The late afternoon sun made a lovely dappled pattern as it shone through the bristling leaves.

35

"I love being in the woods," said Rachel. "You're so lucky to live near a place like this."

The path wound around to the right and the girls saw a huge oak tree with sprawling branches. Some of the branches were so big that they were being propped up by wooden V-shaped crutches. A rope ladder hung down the trunk, and a group of children was standing there, staring up at the treehouse.

"That's Ori," said Kirsty, pointing to the tallest boy.

Ori was wearing a pair of brown trousers and a green T-shirt with a picture of a tree on the front and the words *Treehouse*

*Club* going around the tree in a circle. He had a clipboard. The other children were smaller, but they were wearing the same uniform.

Suddenly, a volley of white balls came flying down from the tree and the children dodged out of the way. As soon as the balls hit the ground, they fell apart.

"Those look like snowballs," said Rachel in an astonished voice. "What are snowballs doing in the forest in the middle of summer?"

# Trouble in the Treehouse

*Whoosh!* A snowball zoomed past Rachel's head and hit the tree behind her. The trunk was suddenly covered in white gloop.

"That's not snow," said Kirsty. "It's marshmallow!"

Dodging through the flying balls of
sticky marshmallow, the girls hurried
over to Ori.

"Are you OK?"
Rachel asked him.
"Who could be
throwing these
things at you?"

"I've been
trying to organise
the Squirrels for
tonight's camp-
out," he replied,
pointing at the younger
children. "But some naughty boys
in the treehouse keep throwing these
sticky, gloopy marshmallows at us. Are
you here to help out?"

Rachel and Kirsty didn't know how to

reply. They couldn't lie, but they couldn't tell him the truth either! Luckily, at that moment some of the Squirrels started throwing bits of sloppy marshmallow back up at the naughty boys. Soon they

were all covered in the gloopy goo.

"We'll never get everything ready at this rate," Ori said, hanging his head. "I wish those boys would stop it. I've tried to talk to them, but they just keep cackling and squawking at me."

Kirsty and Rachel exchanged a knowing glance.

"Cackling and squawking?" said Rachel. "That sounds a bit like someone we know ..."

"Ori, try to stop the Squirrels from throwing marshmallows," said Kirsty. "I've got an idea."

She took Rachel's hand and pulled her deeper into the woods until they reached a grassy clearing. Monica fluttered out of Kirsty's pocket.

"I heard everything," she said. "You

think that they're goblins, don't you?"

"Yes," said Rachel. "And we must get up to that treehouse."

Monica waved her wand, and suddenly the wood seemed much bigger. Rachel and Kirsty were still standing in the clearing, but now the grass seemed as tall

as pine trees.

"We're fairies again," said Kirsty, twirling around and fluttering her wings in delight. "Now we can easily check on the boys in the treehouse."

"Let's be quick," said Rachel. "If they are goblins, they're sure to think of a new

way to make trouble soon."

Together, the three fairies rose into the air and zoomed towards the treehouse, dodging the marshmallows that were flying around them. Kirsty was first.

"There are four windows," she called out. "I can see goblins in three of them."

"Fly towards the fourth window," Monica called. "We mustn't let the goblins see us."

They flew in single file and rose high into the air, and then swooped down to the fourth window. Hovering there, they could see three goblins in the other windows. The goblins were wearing the Treehouse Club

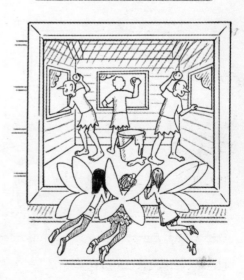

uniform, and were busy throwing gloopy marshmallow balls down at the children as fast as they could.

The long-nosed goblin in the middle window had a huge bucket of gloop beside him. All the goblins were plunging their hands into it to make their marshmallow balls. As the fairies

watched, the gloop ran out.

"I'll try to fill it again," said the long-nosed goblin.

He waved a pink marshmallow over the bucket, and it was instantly full again.

"That's my magical marshmallow," said Monica with a gasp. "We've found it!"

Monica's marshmallow looked more delicious than any marshmallow Rachel and Kirsty had ever seen. It had a magical sparkle and it was perfectly squashy and round.

"Why are the goblins throwing the marshmallow gloop instead of eating it?" Rachel asked. "It's unlike them – they're usually so greedy."

"Goblins only like bogmallows," said Monica. "They're like marshmallows, but green and slimy. They're very smelly.

But goblins love them."

Just then, a gloopy marshmallow ball hurtled towards Rachel and Kirsty. They leaned away from each other and it passed between them. When Kirsty looked at Rachel, she saw her best friend's eyes sparkling.

"I've got an idea," she said with an excited grin. "If the goblins want a marshmallow fight so much, maybe we should let them have one."

The three fairies slipped into the treehouse and each of them scooped up a handful of marshmallow gloop. Staying in the shadows, each of them aimed at a different goblin. Kirsty held up three fingers and counted down. Three, two, one, fire!

Each goblin was hit by a marshmallow

at exactly the same moment. They all
spun around and glared at each other.

"Hey!" squawked one.

"Stop that!" squealed the goblin with
the long nose.

"You'll be sorry, you nit
brains!" the third shouted.

The goblins started
hurling handfuls of
marshmallow gloop
at each other, and

squealing as they were hit. The goblin
with the long nose was still clutching the
magical marshmallow in his hand.

"I'll get it!" Rachel exclaimed.

She swooped towards the goblin, hoping
to pluck the marshmallow out of his
hand. She stretched out her arm, ready
to take the magical sweet. But just before
she reached him, the long-nosed goblin
looked up and saw her.

"Buzz off, you pesky fairy," he yelled.
"It's mine!"

He waved the magical marshmallow
over the bucket.

"It doesn't belong to you," said
Rachel in a gentle voice, hovering in
front of him.

"But I need it," wailed the goblin. "I
want bogmallows now!"

# Smelly Sweets

Monica beckoned Rachel back to her.

"That's what he really wants," she whispered. "Bogmallows! He is trying to use my magical marshmallow to make squishy, smelly bogmallows, but that's not what the magical marshmallow is for. That's why they're coming out so strange and gloopy."

...et the magical ...w back like this," said Kirsty. ...an you turn us back into humans ...gain? I've got an idea."

The three fairies flew back into the woods and landed in the clearing. Then Monica waved her wand and turned Rachel and Kirsty back into humans again.

"Thank you, Monica," said Kirsty. "I know that you need your magical marshmallow to make tasty sweets, but have you got enough magic to make a big bowl of bogmallows?"

"Certainly," said Monica. "With bogmallows, the worse they taste, the more the goblins like them."

She tapped a nearby log with her

wand three times, and a large bowl of green bogmallows appeared in front of them. The smell was so bad that it was making a faint green mist hover over the bowl. Rachel and Kirsty held their noses.

53

"Ugh, it's like rotten eggs and mould and unwashed socks," said Rachel. "How can the goblins *like* them?"

"I don't know," said Kirsty. "But they do – and that might give us a way to get the magical marshmallow back."

Monica slipped back into Kirsty's pocket, and then the girls made their way back to the treehouse with the smelly bogmallows. Ori and the younger children saw them coming, but staggered backwards when they smelled the stench of the bogmallows.

"What is that?" Ori exclaimed,

covering his nose and mouth.

"We've got a way to stop those boys,"
said Rachel. "Trust us."

Ori nodded, and
watched as Rachel
and Kirsty climbed
up the rope ladder
with the bogmallow
bowl. Before they
reached the top,
the goblins had
already smelled the
bogmallows. They were
leaning out over the rope
ladder, licking their lips.

"Give them to us," said the long-nosed
goblin as soon as the girls were in the
treehouse.

"We'd love to," said Kirsty. "All

we want in return
is that marshmallow
you're holding in
your hand."

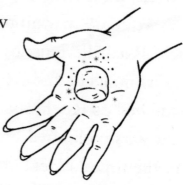

The goblin
glanced down
at the sparkling
magical sweet. The
other two goblins were drooling as the
stench of the bogmallows swirled around
them.

"Jack Frost wouldn't like it ..." said the
long-nosed goblin.

"Jack Frost isn't here," said the second
goblin in an irritated voice. "But a
scrummy bowl of bogmallows is here,
and I want them in my tummy. So hand
over the silly fairy's sweet and let's feast!"

The long-nosed goblin couldn't

resist any more. He shoved the pink
marshmallow into Kirsty's hand, and
snatched the bowl away from her.

"BOGMALLOWS!" boomed the three
goblins, scooping the green, smelly sweets
into their mouths. "YUMMY!"

Monica zoomed out of Kirsty's pocket
and Kirsty handed her the magical
marshmallow. At once, it shrank down
to fairy size.

"This is wonderful!" said Monica, twirling around in mid-air. "Now I can make sure that marshmallows all around the world taste absolutely perfect."

"Jack Frost is going to be very angry," said the long-nosed goblin, sending globs of bogmallow flying out of his mouth as he talked. "But these are so scrumptious that I just don't care."

"Kirsty, let's go back to the van and check Ori's marshmallows," said Rachel in an urgent voice. "We have to make sure that they are back to normal."

Monica hid in Kirsty's pocket again and the girls hurried down the rope ladder. Ori was already organising the Squirrels and helping them to clean the marshmallow goo off their uniforms.

"Thank you for stopping those naughty boys,"

he called out to Rachel and Kirsty.

"No problem," Rachel called to him. "We'll be back in a minute."

The girls ran back down the woodland path until they reached the place where Aunt Harri was still chatting to Carlotta and Calvin. Panting, they darted over to the van, opened the back door and peered into the pink-and-white striped bag. It was full to the brim with fluffy, yummy-looking marshmallows.

"They look perfect," said Kirsty, heaving a huge sigh of relief. "Thank goodness. Now everything is ready for a wonderful Candy Land surprise."

Just then, Aunt Harri turned around and noticed them.

"Hello, girls," she said with a laugh. "Have you come back to check on us? I'm sorry we didn't catch you up — we got distracted talking about our school memories.

Are Ori and the Squirrels ready for the camp-out?"

"I hope so," said Kirsty, smiling. "These marshmallows are ready to be eaten!"

# Helping Hands

When dusk fell, Aunt Harri and the girls were hiding behind the big oak tree. Aunt Harri was holding the bag of marshmallows in her arms. Carlotta, Calvin and Ori were sitting around the campfire with the Squirrels. They sang the Treehouse Club song, and then passed around mugs of frothy hot chocolate.

"This is wonderful," said Ori. "It's exactly what I love best about the Treehouse Club."

"There's just one thing missing," said Carlotta, winking at Calvin.

"I quite agree," said Calvin.

Rachel, Kirsty and Aunt Harri stepped out from behind the big oak tree and walked into the light of the campfire.

"Hello," said Ori. "I wondered where you disappeared to earlier."

"We didn't go far," said Kirsty.

"We've come back because of you," said Rachel, smiling.

Ori looked around at his friends, and they all smiled at him.

"Ori, your friends think you are a very special person," said Aunt Harri. "They have all voted for you to be the first winner of Candy Land's Helping Hands award. Congratulations, here is your prize."

She handed the bag to Ori, who gasped in delight when he peeped inside.

"My favourites!" he said, going pink with pleasure. "Thank you."

"Thank you for all your help with the Squirrels and the Treehouse Club," said Calvin, shaking his hand.

Rachel nudged Kirsty and pointed at the oak tree. The three goblins had come down the rope and were watching, still stuffing bogmallows into their mouths.

"I'd like to share these with everyone," said Ori, passing the bag around the group of excited Squirrels.

"We can toast them on the fire for you," said Carlotta.

The Squirrels cheered, and Ori noticed
the goblins standing nearby.

"You can have some too, if you would
like," he said. "There's
enough for everyone."

The goblins
were still in their
Treehouse Club
uniforms, so Ori
thought they were
ordinary boys.

"We've got
some," squawked
the long-nosed
goblin awkwardly.
"But ... er ... thanks."

They came and joined the group
around the fire. A few of the Squirrels
moved away from the smell of the

bogmallows, but they still made the goblins welcome.

"It's nice to see the goblins enjoying themselves," said Kirsty in a low voice. "That's another good deed that Ori's done for others."

Dusk had passed now, and night had fallen. The moon was shining brightly, giving the treehouse a soft glow.

"The treehouse looks almost magical, doesn't it," said Aunt Harri, noticing the girls staring at it.

Rachel and Kirsty exchanged a secret smile.

"May we go up to the top, Aunt Harri?" Kirsty asked.

"Yes, as long as you're careful," said Aunt Harri.

Once again, the girls climbed up the swinging rope ladder to the treehouse. It was even more exciting to be up there in the moonlight. As soon as they were inside, Monica flew out of Rachel's pocket.

"Thank you both so

much for your help," she said. "I'm glad I stayed long enough to see Ori get his award. I want to give you both a treat too – something to say thank you for all you have done."

She waved her wand and a bowl of fluffy marshmallows appeared on the treehouse floor. Monica hovered above the bowl, and the moonlight made her wings glimmer.

"Pick up a marshmallow," she said, smiling. "I'm going to show you how to make taffy."

Monica showed the girls how to twist the marshmallows using just their fingertips, and then pull them apart.

"Now press them together, and twist and pull again," said Monica. "Keep going."

Slowly, the mixture stopped coming apart. It stretched between their fingers, a soft and glossy new type of candy.

"This is fun," said Rachel, giggling as she watched the marshmallows change.

"Fun *and* delicious," said Monica. "I hope you enjoy eating it. Thank you again. I must return to Fairyland."

"Please tell the other Candy Land Fairies that they can count on us," said Kirsty. Rachel nodded.

Monica smiled, and then she was gone in a puff of silvery fairy dust. Rachel and Kirsty popped pieces of taffy into their mouths and shared a hug.

"I'm so glad that we could help

Monica to get her magical marshmallow back from Jack Frost and the goblins," said Rachel. "I just hope that we can help the other Candy Land Fairies too."

"We can't let Jack Frost ruin the rest of the Candy Land's Helping Hands treats," said Kirsty. "And we mustn't let the Harvest Feast be a disaster either."

"Then we have more magical adventures ahead," said Rachel with a sparkle in her eyes. "It's going to be an exciting week!"

The End

**Now it's time for Kirsty and
Rachel to help ...**

# Gabby the Bubble Gum Fairy

**Read on for a sneak peek ...**

Rachel Walker whizzed down the candy-cane slide. She squealed with laughter as she zoomed off the end on to a trampoline and bounced into the air.

"This is the best park in the whole wide world," she called to her best friend, Kirsty Tate, who was sitting at the top of the slide.

"WHEEEEEE!" Kirsty sang out as she shot down the slide and bounced down beside Rachel. "It's so much fun. I'm so glad that Aunt Harri asked us to meet her here."

Rachel was staying with Kirsty for a

whole week. It was always fun visiting Wetherbury, but this time it was extra exciting. Kirsty's Aunt Harri, who worked at the Candy Land sweet factory, had asked the girls to help her with some very special deliveries. Candy Land was giving out Helping Hands awards for people who were doing wonderful things to help the community. It was part of Aunt Harri's job to present the winners with bags of their favourite sweets, and Rachel and Kirsty were proud to help.

"I expect your Aunt Harri will be here soon," said Rachel, checking her watch.

The girls stopped bouncing and looked over at the factory. The sweet-themed park was in the beautiful grounds of the factory, on the outskirts of Wetherbury. The tall slide looked as if it had been made from candy canes, the swings were shaped like jelly beans and the roundabout looked like a circle of liquorice. On the far side of the park, some boys were playing by a fence that seemed to be made of strawberry laces.

Just then, Kirsty noticed a little boy sitting on one end of the seesaw, which was shaped like a stick of rock.

"That little boy looks sad," she said. "I wonder if he is lonely. Maybe one of us should go and sit on the other end of the seesaw so he can have a turn."

"I think someone else has already had that idea," said Rachel.

A girl with long brown hair was walking towards the seesaw, smiling. She said something to the little boy, and a smile lit up his face. Then she sat on the other end of the seesaw and started to go up and down.

"What a kind girl," said Kirsty. "I noticed her earlier, pushing a little girl on the swings."

When the little boy's mum called him away, the girl left the seesaw and walked towards Rachel and Kirsty.

"Hi," she said in a friendly voice. "I haven't seen you here before. I'm Olivia. I'm the playground buddy for this park."

Read **Gabby the Bubble Gum Fairy** to find out what adventures are in store for Kirsty and Rachel!

# RAINBOW magic

**Calling all parents, carers and teachers!**
The Rainbow Magic fairies are here to help
your child enter the magical world of reading.
Whatever reading stage they are at, there's
a Rainbow Magic book for everyone!
Here is Lydia the Reading Fairy's guide to
supporting your child's journey at all levels.

## Starting Out

Our Rainbow Magic Beginner Readers are perfect for first-time readers who are just beginning to develop reading skills and confidence. Approved by teachers, they contain a full range of educational levelling, as well as lively full-colour illustrations.

## Developing Readers

Rainbow Magic Early Readers contain longer stories and wider vocabulary for building stamina and growing confidence. These are adaptations of our most popular Rainbow Magic stories, specially developed for younger readers in conjunction with an Early Years reading consultant, with full-colour illustrations.

## Going Solo

The Rainbow Magic chapter books – a mixture of series and one-off specials – contain accessible writing to encourage your child to venture into reading independently. These highly collectible and much-loved magical stories inspire a love of reading to last a lifetime.

www.rainbowmagicbooks.co.uk

"Rainbow Magic got my daughter reading chapter books. Great sparkly covers, cute fairies and traditional stories full of magic that she found impossible to put down" - Mother of Edie (6 years)

"Florence LOVES the Rainbow Magic books. She really enjoys reading now" - Mother of Florence (6 years)

# The Rainbow Magic Reading Challenge

Well done, fairy friend – you have completed the book!
**This book was worth 10 points.**

See how far you have climbed on the
**Reading Rainbow** opposite.

The more books you read, the more points you will get,
and the closer you will be to becoming a Fairy Princess!

**Do you want your own Reading Rainbow?**
1. Cut out the coin below
2. Go to the Rainbow Magic website
3. Download and print out your poster
4. Add your coin and climb up the Reading Rainbow!

There's all this and lots more at
**www.rainbowmagicbooks.co.uk**

You'll find activities, competitions, stories, a special
newsletter and complete profiles of all the
Rainbow Magic fairies. Find a fairy with your name!